A NOTE TO PARENTS

One of the most important ways children learn to read — and learn to *like* reading — is by being with readers. Every time you read aloud, read along, or listen to your child read, you are providing the support that she or he needs as an emerging reader.

Disney's First Readers were created to make that reading time fun for you and your child. Each book in this series features characters that most children already recognize from popular Disney films. The familiarity and appeal of these high-interest characters will draw emerging readers easily into the story and at the same time support basic literacy skills, such as understanding that print has meaning, connecting oral language to written language, and developing cueing systems. And because Disney's First Readers are highly visual, children have another tool to help in understanding the text. This makes early reading a comfortable, confident experience — exactly what emerging readers need to become successful, fluent readers.

Read to Your Child

Here are a few hints to make early reading enjoyable and educational:

★ Talk with children before reading. Let them see how much they already know about the Disney characters. If they are unfamiliar with the movie basis of a book, take a few minutes to look at the cover and some of the illustrations to establish a context. Talking is important, since oral language precedes and supports reading.

★ Run your finger along the text to show that the words carry the story. Let your child read along if she or he recognizes that there are repeated words or phrases.

★ Encourage questions. A child's questions are good clues to his or her comprehension or thinking strategies.

★ Be prepared to read the same book several times. Children will develop ease with the story and concepts, so that later they can concentrate on reading and language.

Let Your Child Read to You

You are your child's best audience, so encourage her or him to read aloud to you often. And:

★ If children ask about an unknown word, give it to them. Don't interrupt the flow of reading to have them sound it out. However, if children start to sound out a word, let them.

★ Praise all reading efforts warmly and often!

— Patricia Koppman
Past President
International Reading Association

Pencils by Denise Shimabukoro

Printed in the United States of America.

1   3   5   7   9   10   8   6   4   2

Library of Congress Catalog Card Number: 96-85712

ISBN 0-7868-4075-7

Where's Flit?

by Bettina Ling

Illustrated by Eric Binder
and Darren Hont

Disney's First Readers — Level 1
A Story from Disney's *Pocahontas*

New York

"Let's go see Grandmother Willow,"
Pocahontas calls to Flit and Meeko.

"There's the path.
Come on, let's go."

As Meeko leads the way,
Pocahontas stops to say,
"Where's Flit?"

Here's a good place to hide.
Pocahontas looks inside.

No Flit.

Pocahontas looks in a tree.
What's up there?
Whose nest does she see?

Not Flit's.

Meeko hears a sound.
He looks all around.

No Flit.

Is Flit down a hole?

Or inside the log?

Or under the mud
with one tiny frog?

When Pocahontas reaches water,
she sees fish and an otter.

But no Flit.

Where else can they look?
Where else can they go?

Maybe Grandmother Willow
will know.

Pocahontas leads the way.
She is just about to say,
"Where's Flit?"